The Snow Globe

Jean Ure

With illustrations by
Charlie Alder

12724062

For Mae McLoughlin

First published in 2016 in Great Britain by
Barrington Stoke Ltd
18 Walker Street, Edinburgh, EH3 7LP

www.barringtonstoke.co.uk

Text © 2016 Jean Ure
Illustrations © 2016 Charlie Alder

The moral right of Jean Ure and Charlie Alder to be
identified as the author and illustrator of this work has
been asserted in accordance with the Copyright, Designs
and Patents Act, 1988

All rights reserved. No part of this publication may be
reproduced in whole or in any part in any form without
the written permission of the publisher

A CIP catalogue record for this book is available
from the British Library upon request

ISBN: 978-1-78112-594-6

Printed in Great Britain by Charlesworth Press

Contents

1 Happy Holidays   1

2 Welcome to Gladeside   8

3 New Best Friends   16

4 Someone Special   23

5 Big Brothers, Little Brothers   29

6 A Broken Promise   41

7 Second Thoughts   51

8 What's the Secret?   59

9 Real Friends   67

Chapter 1
Happy Holidays

Once upon a time, my mum and dad ran their own business. It was called Happy Holidays and it had a website – happyholidays.com. The website was full of pictures of sandy beaches and bright blue sea. I used to enjoy going on it to read the messages people had left.

Had a fab time!

The surf was amazing!

The team at Happy Holidays really go the extra mile!

Back then, we lived in a house called Chimneys with an in-and-out drive at the front and a big garden at the back. There was Mum and Dad and me, and my baby brother Jax. We had a double garage for Mum's and Dad's cars and I went to school at Lady Margaret Foster's. I was in my first year there and I had a best friend, Jenny. Jenny and I had been friends since primary school. We went to dance classes together and did horse riding at the weekend. Life was fun! Like a happy holiday all of my own. I thought it would go on for ever ... But then, all of a sudden, it came to a full stop.

I'll never forget the day Mum told me. It was a Saturday morning, near the end of the spring term. Mum came into my bedroom and pulled back the curtains. Then she sat down on the edge of my bed. She was looking very grave.

"Abi, there's something I have to tell you," she said. "We've put it off as long as we could, but it's finally happened ... Happy Holidays has gone under."

I didn't get it at first. I crinkled my brow. "You mean ..."

"It's run out of money," Mum said. "Your dad and I have to wind everything down."

I couldn't understand it. How could Happy Holidays run out of money? What about all the happy holiday-makers?

Mum sighed. "These things happen," she said. "But I'm afraid, Abs, we're going to have to make some changes."

I listened in silence while Mum told me what those changes were going to be. First of all we were going to have to sell the house and rent one in a different part of town. Also,

Mum told me, I would have to give up my riding lessons and maybe my dance classes as well.

"Just until we find our feet again," she said.

I didn't mind so much about the riding lessons. To be honest, I only did them to keep up with Jenny. I didn't even mind that much about the dance classes. But I was really shocked when Mum said I would have to leave Lady Margaret's.

"Leave *Lady Margaret's?*" I said.

"I know," said Mum, "I'm so sorry. I know you love it there. But it would be far too long a journey every day. Right across town ... it would take for ever."

I felt my lips begin to quiver.

Mum said, "Oh, Abs, try to be brave. Your dad and I feel so bad about everything. I know it's hard on you, I know it's asking a lot, but ..."

Her voice trailed away. I swallowed. I thought how Mum and Dad must be feeling. They had worked so hard. And now it was all falling apart.

"I expect I'll get used to it," I mumbled.

"That's a girl," Mum said. "You'll make new friends in no time. You'll see!"

On Monday I had to break the news to Jenny. I didn't tell her that Happy Holidays had gone under. I just said that Mum and Dad had decided to sell the house and that I would be going to a new school.

I waited for her to cry, "Oh, Abi, no!" After all, we *were* best friends. But all she said was, "Where are you going to go?"

"Mum's talking about somewhere called Gladeside," I said.

"Never heard of it," said Jenny. "What's it like?"

"Well … it's quite big," I said. I'd looked it up on the internet. "Oh, and it has boys," I added.

We didn't have any boys at Lady Margaret's. I wasn't sure whether they were a good thing or a bad thing.

Jenny pulled a face. "I bet you'll hate it," she said.

Chapter 2
Welcome to Gladeside

The new house that we moved to was a lot smaller than our old one. It was so small that we couldn't get everything in and we had to sell lots of stuff. Even Dapple, the old rocking horse that Gran had given me. We didn't even have room for Dapple! Gran wasn't here any more, so it did make me a bit sad to say goodbye to him.

"Abi, I'm so sorry," Dad said.

I promised him that I didn't really mind. I was too old for rocking horses anyway, and Jax was just a baby. He couldn't even sit on Dapple unless I was there to hold him.

"I'm afraid this house is like a biscuit tin," Dad said, as we lugged some more boxes upstairs.

"I think it's cosy," I said.

Dad hugged me. "Thank you for being so brave."

I wasn't really brave. In a few weeks I would be starting the new summer term at Gladeside. Every time I thought about it I felt all shaky. Jenny didn't help. She said that she had looked it up on the internet too.

"It's *huge*," she said. "You'll totally hate it!"

She kept telling me over and over. It was all she could talk about. How Gladeside was huge and I would totally HATE it.

9

At the end of term we said goodbye to each other and promised that we would keep in touch.

"You'll have to come for a sleepover," I said.

Jenny agreed that she would. But even before the end of term she had started to hang out with other people. It was like we had already stopped being friends.

When the time came for me to go to Gladeside, it was Dad who took me in. It seemed odd for Dad to be at home instead of at work. I knew that he was looking very hard for a job. Mum said that maybe they would be able to start another business, but until then, Dad had to go out and earn some money. And I had to come to this big, scary school!

Dad came with me to the Office and handed me over to Miss Andrews, one of the school secretaries. Miss Andrews smiled and said, "Welcome to Gladeside. Abi Castillo, is it?"

I just nodded. My mouth had gone dry and I couldn't speak. Dad gave my hand a squeeze.

"See you later," he said. "All right?"

No! It wasn't all right! I felt desperate. I wanted to scream, "Dad, please don't leave me!" But of course I didn't cos I was twelve years old and you don't behave like that when you're twelve years old. You have to pretend not to be scared.

Miss Andrews took me down a corridor and up some stairs and down another corridor and up some steps and through some double doors and down yet another corridor until I was completely lost. How was I ever going to find my way around?

"Here we are," Miss Andrews said. "7C. This is you."

She opened the door. I couldn't believe it! The classroom was full! A huge great crowd of kids, all shouting and yelling. They were banging on their desk tops, clattering up and down. Nobody ever did that at Lady Margaret's.

"Ah, here's Mrs Hicks!" Miss Andrews said. She sounded a bit relieved. "Mrs Hicks, this is Abi Castillo. I'll leave her in your care."

I guessed that Mrs Hicks was the class teacher. The noise stopped as soon as she came in. This was because she slapped a book on her desk and bellowed, "QUIET, THE LOT OF YOU!" I had never heard a teacher bellow before. Not even Ms Crowe, our old PE teacher at Lady Margaret's. The most Ms Crowe ever did was clap her hands and cry, "Come along, girls! Get a move on!" I didn't think this lot would take much notice of Ms Crowe. Some of them were still talking even now.

Mrs Hicks sent me to a desk at the front, next to a big, angry-looking girl. I wondered if she was angry because of me, like maybe she would have preferred to sit with one of her friends. I tried smiling at her, but she just glared so after that I kept my head bent over my desk and didn't look at her. At the end of the first lesson she leaned across and said, "So where did you go before?"

I guessed she meant which school was I at. I said, "Lady Margaret Foster."

"Oh," she said, in a silly sing-song voice, "Lady Margaret *Foster*. Where's that, then? Somewhere posh?"

There was a sudden silence. I could feel everyone staring. My cheeks began to sizzle.

"It's just an ordinary school," I muttered.

It wasn't big, it wasn't posh. But I'd been happy there. Jenny was right. I was never going to be happy at Gladeside. It was a horrible, horrible school!

Chapter 3
New Best Friends

At break I followed everyone outside and stood in a corner, by myself. I hated this school. I hated everything about it. All the big, tough boys and the loud, shouting girls. Teachers that bellowed. And the uniform! I even hated the uniform. At Lady Margaret Foster's we had worn tartan skirts and red blazers with 'LMF' on the pocket. At Gladeside it was grey. Plain, boring *grey*.

As I stood there in the playground, I felt tears prick the back of my eyes. I blinked them away. *I was not going to cry!* Maybe it would help if I wandered round. I would put on my best bright smile so that nobody would know how alone I felt.

I was just about to set off when a girl came skipping up to me. I'd seen her in class. She was small and bouncy and bursting with energy.

"Hey!" she said.

I said, "Hey."

"I'm Millie," she said. "You're the new girl, aren't you? What's your name?"

"Abi," I said.

"Hi, Abi!" She held out a hand, like she expected me to shake it. "Do you want to be friends?"

I felt my heart do a great happy leap. "Yes, all right," I said.

I didn't really know who she was, any more than she knew who I was. But she wanted to be friends. She linked her arm with mine.

"We'll be a pair," she said. "You 'n' me! Let's walk round together and show them."

I wasn't sure who we were showing, but the tears had stopped pricking and I was suddenly feeling happy. Millie pointed people out to me as we walked.

"That girl over there, the one with the pointy nose ... that's Nina Kirkby," she said. "She's mean! Nobody likes her. And that one, in the corner, that's Opal. She's OK. Just a bit odd."

I thought Opal looked a bit sad. She was standing all by herself. She was very pale and

sort of hunched, like she was trying to make herself invisible.

"See that boy there?" Millie said. "The one kicking a ball? That's Colm O'Leary. Everybody's got a crush on him. Well, everybody except me. And that's his cousin ... Marie McKenna. She's really popular."

I asked Millie about the girl I'd sat next to.

"You mean Dahlia," she said.

"Yes," I said. "I think she's cross about something."

"Dahlia's always cross," Millie said. "You don't want to worry about her. I'll ask Mrs Hicks if we can change seats."

Mrs Hicks was the teacher who'd bellowed. I was quite surprised when Millie said that she was really nice. "She won't mind if we swop over," she said.

"What about Dahlia?" I asked.

"Oh, it won't bother her," said Millie.

Millie was right. She asked Dahlia as soon as we were back in class and Dahlia just said, "Yeah, whatever," and took herself off to Millie's old seat.

"*That's* better," said Millie.

Gladeside didn't seem nearly so bad now that I had a friend. I didn't think of my old school once all the rest of the day. Mum and Dad would be so pleased when they heard about Millie. It would stop them worrying quite so much. I couldn't wait for the end of school so I could tell them ...

But then, just as I was about to go out of the gates to where Dad was waiting for me, Millie came running up.

"Hey, Abi," she said. "You know I asked you if you wanted to be friends?"

My heart sank. She was going to tell me she'd changed her mind!

"D'you want to be *best* friends?" said Millie.

Chapter 4
Someone Special

On Wednesday when I got home from school, Mum said, "Do you have a girl called Nina in your class?"

"Nina Kirkby," I said. She was the one with the pointy nose. The one Millie had said was mean.

"Nina Kirkby," said Mum. "That's the one. I bumped into her mum while I was out this morning. She was telling me how Nina only started at Gladeside last term. It seems she's not very happy there."

I hadn't been very happy earlier in the week. Now I was friends with Millie, it had made all the difference.

"I told her that you were still very new," Mum said. "I suggested that maybe you and Nina might become friends. What do you think?"

I pulled a face. "I've already got a friend," I said. "I've got Millie."

"Yes, I know, and I'm so pleased," said Mum. "But there's nothing to stop you having more than one friend, is there?"

I didn't want more than one! Not if it meant I had to be friends with Nina Kirkby. Millie was right – she was mean. Only yesterday I'd heard her saying really nasty things about some of the other girls in our year.

Mum said, "I was thinking maybe you could ask her to tea some time."

"*Mum!*" I said. I was horrified.

"Well, why not?" said Mum. "She only lives a few minutes away. But if you think it's too soon to ask her over, you could at least go and talk to her."

"What am I supposed to talk about?" I said.

"Anything," said Mum. "Just give it a go!"

Mum could see from my face that I didn't like the idea. She sighed. "Well, I won't push you," she said. "But at least think about it. Will you?"

I promised that I would, so I did. But I still didn't like the idea.

Next day at break I told Millie about it. "My mum bumped into Nina's mum and they got talking," I said. "And now my mum wants me to be friends with her!"

"With Nina?" said Millie. "Yuck! You're not going to, are you?"

I shook my head very hard. "No way!"

"Cos she's really mean," said Millie. "And anyway, we're a pair."

"I know," I said. "It's what I told Mum ... and then she said she wanted me to invite her to tea!"

"She wouldn't if she knew what Nina was like. She's really spiteful," Millie said. "Last term she went round telling everyone that

Kevin Watkins wasn't right in the head. Just cos he can be a bit slow sometimes. It was really unkind. But that's what she's like. I think you should tell your mum," said Millie. "Then she'll know why you don't want to be friends with her."

"Mm." I considered the idea. I'd once grumbled to Mum about a girl at Lady Margaret's who liked to be mean behind people's backs, and Mum had said maybe she was just unhappy and I should give her a chance. She might say that about Nina.

"You could always ask *me* to tea," Millie said. "And then I could ask you back. Please, *please!* Have *me* to tea!"

"I'll ask Mum," I said.

I asked Mum as soon as I got home from school. "Yes, of course you can invite Millie," she said. "Why not invite Nina, as well?"

I took a deep breath and blurted it out. "Cos I don't like her very much."

"Oh, Abi! You don't even know her," Mum said. "You've only been at the school a few days. Did you go and talk to her?"

"Not yet," I muttered.

"Then how can you say you don't like her?"

"Mum, *please*," I said. "Can't it just be Millie?"

Mum shook her head, like, *Oh, I give up!*

"This Millie must be someone very special," she said.

"She is," I said. "She's my best friend."

Chapter 5
Big Brothers, Little Brothers

"So you're the famous Millie," Dad said, when Millie arrived on Saturday afternoon. "We've heard lots of good things about you!"

"*Dad!*" I said.

Parents really can be quite embarrassing at times. But Millie didn't seem to mind. She said, "Me and Abi are best friends."

"So I gather," said Dad. "Well, bring her in then, Abi. Don't keep her standing on the doorstep."

"Come and say hello to Mum and Jax," I said, "then we can go up to my room."

"Jax is *so* sweet," Millie said, as we went upstairs.

"Oh, do you think so?" I said. A bit earlier on, he had been *very* annoying. He had kept running at me and clutching my legs.

"I wish I had a baby brother," said Millie.

"You've got a *big* brother," I said.

Millie's brother was called Eddie. He had driven her here in his van. I bet *he* wasn't annoying.

"Oh, is this your bedroom?" Millie cried. "It's lovely!"

I was surprised she said that. My old bedroom had been lovely. This one was quite small and poky.

"Look at all your little dogs and cats!" Millie had rushed over to the mantelpiece, where I kept all my china ornaments lined up. Not just dogs and cats but a dormouse and a pony and a white rabbit, as well.

"And look at all your books! Oh, you're so lucky."

"You can borrow some, if you like," I said.

But Millie had already raced across to my dressing table and was picking things up and exclaiming over them. The tiny little scent bottle that had belonged to Gran, the china donkey with long ears poking out of his straw hat, the cow made out of soap that I'd had for years and couldn't bring myself to use.

"Everything is just so lovely," Millie said.

Jenny had never said everything was so lovely. She had never said that anything was lovely at all. It was good to have a friend who liked my things so much.

"What about this?" I said. I picked up my snow globe, with its little house, and held it out to her.

"Oh!" Millie's eyes opened wide. "That is *so* beautiful."

"You can hold it, if you want," I said. "See what happens when you shake it ..."

She shook it, and laughed in delight as flakes of snow began to fall over the little house.

"My gran made it for me," I said.

Millie held it cupped in both hands. "It's the most beautiful thing I've ever seen," she said. "I wish I could show it to my mum. Maybe you

could bring it with you when you come to my place ... would your mum let you?"

"I don't see why not," I said. "When shall I come?"

"Saturday?" said Millie. "Come next Saturday!"

"All right," I said. "I'll see if that's OK."

I meant to check with Mum when we went back downstairs, but Mum was on the phone and I forgot all about it.

"Can we go in the garden?" Millie said.

"Of course you can," said Dad.

Jax insisted on coming with us. Jenny always said that Jax was a pain and got in the way, but Millie just dumped him in the wheelbarrow and whizzed him off across the grass, yelling, "Roman chariot! All hail!"

It got Jax a bit over-excited. It made him scream and bounce up and down so that in the end Millie lost control and the wheelbarrow went hurtling madly across a flower bed and crashed into the fence. Jax thought it was great fun.

"Again!" he cried. "Do again!"

"I don't think we'd better," I said. I could see a jagged hole in the fence where the wheelbarrow had bashed into it. "I think we'd better go in, now, and have tea."

"So did you have fun out there?" Mum said.

Jax said, "Yes! Me and Millie played chariots."

Mum looked pleased. *She* knew that Jenny had never played with Jax. She said, "That was nice of you, Millie."

Now I was pleased, too. I did so much want Mum to approve. Maybe now she would stop trying to make me be friends with that horrible Nina. Things were looking good!

But then, when we sat down to tea, Jax had to go and ruin everything. He pointed at Millie. "Got elbows on table," he said.

I felt like whacking him with a spoon. Mum and Dad are really old-fashioned about table manners. It's always –

Don't slurp!

Don't talk with your mouth full!

Don't put your elbows on the table!

How was Millie to know?

"Jax, hush!" said Mum.

Millie turned bright red.

It was Dad who saved the day. He said, "You just worry about your own elbows, my boy!"

After tea, Dad went into the garden to put something in the bin. When he came back he wasn't looking very pleased.

"What happened to the fence?" he said.

This time it was me that went red. "Sorry," I mumbled. "It was an accident."

"It wasn't Abi's fault," Millie said. "It was me."

"She was playing with Jax," I said. I thought if I said that it would stop them being cross.

Dad said, "Oh. Well. All right, then! So long as we know."

I could tell that he still wasn't too happy. Mum didn't look all that happy either.

There was an uneasy silence. It seemed to go on for ever. Then Mum said, a bit too brightly, "Why don't we have a game of Monopoly?"

"Ooh, yes," Millie cried, "I love Monopoly!"

Everything was going great until Millie got sent to Jail – *Go directly to Jail. Do not pass Go* – and shouted "*Damn!*" at the top of her voice. There was another horrible silence. I saw Mum and Dad exchange glances. Then Dad said, "Now, now, young lady! We'll have none of that."

Bad language is another thing that Mum and Dad are a bit old-fashioned about. Well, what *they* call bad language. I felt like crawling under the table and not coming out.

At six o'clock we packed the Monopoly away and Mum said, "So, is someone coming to pick you up, Millie?"

"Yep." Millie nodded. "My brother."

Even as she said it there was the sound of a horn honking in the road outside.

"Oh!" Millie jumped up. "That'll be him now!"

My heart sank. This was getting worse and worse! One of Dad's pet hates is when people sit and honk their horns.

We all went to the front door. A van was parked half on and half off the kerb.

"Is that him?" Dad said, rather grimly.

Millie beamed. "Yes!" she said. "That's Eddie."

Eddie leaned across the passenger seat and shouted at us through the open window. "Sorry, mate! Couldn't find anywhere to park."

I didn't dare to look at Dad.

But Millie gave Jax a hug, then turned to Mum and said, "Thank you so much for the lovely tea and I'm really sorry about the fence."

That made me feel better. Jenny had never said thank you for the lovely tea! Of course she had never crashed a wheelbarrow into the fence, either. But then *she* had never played Roman chariots with Jax.

Chapter 6
A Broken Promise

At school on Monday our English teacher, Ms Hussain, said, "For homework I'd like you to write a few sentences about some object that's important to you. We can then read out what you've written and see if people can guess what the object is. Oh, and do bring it to school with you so that we can all see it."

"*What* is it we've got to bring to school?" Kevin said, as Ms Hussain left the room at the end of class.

"An object," Nina snapped.

Kevin looked puzzled. "What's an object?" he said.

Nina rolled her eyes. "Something! Anything! A lump of mud, if you want."

She was being really mean. Kevin worked hard and he was such a sweet boy. *He* never did anything to hurt people.

Just bring something that you like," Millie said, kindly. And then she tugged at my arm. "You could bring your you-know-what!"

She meant Gran's snow globe. I was tempted. "But you'd know what it was," I said.

"That's all right," said Millie. "I wouldn't tell. And you will bring it on Saturday, won't you? Cos I want my mum to see it."

Oh. I clapped a hand to my mouth. I still hadn't asked Mum about Saturday. I'd completely forgotten.

"What's the matter?" said Millie.

I couldn't tell her! I felt too bad about it.

"I hope Kevin finds something to bring," I said. "I feel so sorry for him."

"It's her," said Millie. "That Nina. She's so mean to him. If it happens again I'll report her. I don't care if it's telling tales! She deserves it."

That day, at the end of school, I found I was walking up the road with Nina. Mum had said I could get the bus, now that I knew my way round. Unfortunately, it seemed that Nina got the same bus as I did.

"I don't know *why* you hang around with that Millie," she said, as we waited at the bus stop.

"Cos I'm friends with her," I said. "That's why."

Nina tossed her head. "You won't be for long. Your mum won't let you. She tried to be friends with me when I first came, but my mum soon put a stop to it."

I was going to ask her why, but at that moment the bus came. I was hoping it would be crowded cos I really *really* didn't want to sit with Nina, but there was an empty seat at the back and she crammed herself down next to me.

"I'm surprised *your* mum hasn't put a stop to it," she said. "Millie's not at all a nice person. You know where she lives, don't you?"

"No," I said. "Where?"

"Tanner's Fields," Nina said. "It's this big estate. She wanted me to go there one time for tea, but my mum wouldn't let me. I wouldn't have gone anyway. Mum says it's where they put the problem families."

I turned away and stared, very hard, out of the window.

"Has she asked you yet?" Nina said.

"Yes." I nodded. "As a matter of fact, I'm going there on Saturday."

"That's what you think," said Nina.

I turned slowly back to look at her.

"Your mum will never let you," she said. "You'll see."

It was all a bit worrying. As soon as I arrived home I said to Mum, "Is it OK if I go to Millie's on Saturday?"

I was really shocked when Mum said no.

"But, Mum," I said, "I promised her."

"I'm sorry," said Mum, "you should have checked with me first. I spoke to Nina's mum again this morning. She's invited us to the Summer Fair at her little boy's school. I thought we should see what it's like, in case Jax goes there."

"So why do I have to come?" I said. *I* didn't care what the stupid school was like. "Why can't I just go to Millie's?"

Mum pursed her lips. "To be honest, Abi, I'm not too happy with you and Millie being friends. I'm sure she means well, but ..."

"*What?*" I said.

"There's no need to be rude," said Mum.

I said, "I'm not being rude! But if it's cos of where she lives –"

"Yes," Mum said. "Nina's mum was telling me. She says Tanner's Fields has a very bad reputation."

I said, "Millie can't help where she lives."

"No, but she can help the sort of language she uses," said Mum.

I said, "Oh, *please*! All she said was damn."

"I'd still rather she didn't say it," said Mum. "I'd rather you didn't, either."

"*Damn* isn't anything!" I said it scornfully. How little Mum knew. "You should hear the boys in my class ... they say far worse things than that!"

"Maybe so," Mum said. "But you don't have to be friends with them. In the meantime, I've told Nina's mum we'll go along on Saturday and that is that."

※

Next morning I had to break the news to Millie. She came bouncing over, all bright and beaming. And then I told her that I couldn't come on Saturday and her face fell. I didn't tell her that Mum didn't approve of her, but it seemed like she guessed anyway. Maybe she was used to mums not approving.

I felt really bad. Millie was my best friend. It didn't help that Nina had to come and stick her pointy nose in. "It'll be ever such fun on Saturday," she said. "I'm really looking forward to it."

So then, of course, I had to tell Millie about the stupid Summer Fair. I could see that she was hurt.

"Your mum and dad don't like me, do they?" she said.

"It's not that they don't *like* you," I said, "but you shouldn't have used that word –"

"What word?" said Millie.

"You know what word!" I said.

"You mean damn?" said Millie. She tossed her head. "I can say damn if I want … I can say it as much as I like. Damn damn *damn*!"

With that she went running off to join Marie McKenna and a group of other girls. We didn't talk any more all the rest of the day.

Chapter 7
Second Thoughts

"Abi, for goodness sake," Mum said. "Do try to look a bit happier."

I pulled a face. It was Saturday afternoon and we were on our way to meet Nina and her mum. How was I supposed to look happy?

"Just take that look off your face," Mum said. "Stop sulking!"

I wasn't sulking. I was miserable. I had hurt my best friend and now she was refusing to talk to me.

"This is a chance for you and Nina to get to know each other," said Mum.

I didn't want us to know each other. I already knew everything I needed to know about Nina Kirkby. She was mean!

Her mum was mean, as well. "I gather you had trouble with that girl ... Millie, or whatever her name is," she said.

She wasn't talking to me, she was talking to Mum. But I could hear her.

"I'm afraid there are a lot of girls like that at Gladeside. It's a very rough sort of school. Nina's had such a hard time. It's not what she's used to. She was at St John's before, you know. St John's is very select."

I wasn't 100% positive what *select* meant, but Mrs Kirkby seemed to think it was a good thing. Mum didn't sound so sure.

"Abi seems to have settled down really well at Gladeside," she said.

"I just HATE it," said Nina. "That awful girl they made Abi sit next to on her first day … that *Dahlia*." She shuddered.

"Dahlia's all right," I said.

Nina sniffed. "She should be got rid of, if you ask me. *And* Kevin Watkins." She turned to Mum and Mrs Kirkby, who were walking behind us. "You'll never believe it," she said. "He asked me the other day what an *object* was!"

Mrs Kirkby shook her head. "It's not right," she said. "The slow ones hold everybody up. We're thinking of sending Nina somewhere private instead."

'Oh,' I thought, 'I wish you would.'

"I expect you miss your old school, don't you, Abi?" Nina's mum looked at me hopefully, like she really wanted me to say yes.

I stopped to think about it. I had to begin with, but not any more. Not now that I had got used to being with boys, and I had stopped being scared of Dahlia, and I had learned how to find my way round. I didn't even miss Jenny as much as I'd thought I would.

Mum was looking worried. She said, "You wouldn't want to go back to Lady Margaret's, would you, Abi?"

"Not now," I said. "I quite like it where I am."

If only Millie would talk to me!

Mum was quiet on the way home. I was quiet, too. I was thinking of Millie. And then

Mum turned to me. "Abi, I've been having second thoughts," she said. "I was wrong to stop you and Millie seeing each other. I can understand why you don't want to be friends with Nina. I don't want you to be friends with Nina either. I'm so sorry I tried to push you."

I think my mouth must have fallen open. Mum laughed.

"Don't look so surprised!" she said. "Mums can make mistakes just the same as anyone else. Why don't you ask Millie if she'd like to come for a sleepover some time?"

Mum made it sound so easy. She didn't know how hurt Millie was feeling.

I muttered that I would try.

"First thing Monday," said Mum.

I didn't do it first thing. I waited till the lunch break so I could get my courage up. She still wouldn't talk to me.

"Millie –" I began. But she was off and away before I could even get the words out. I watched, sadly, as she stood laughing with Marie and her friends. Nina came up to me, all gloating and full of triumph.

"I told you, didn't I?" she said. "I said your mum wouldn't let you be friends with her."

"Oh, go boil yourself!" I snapped and I walked away, very fast, across the playground. Opal was there, standing by herself in a corner. Her face lit up when she saw me.

"Have you and Millie stopped being friends?" she said.

I made a grunting sound. Not quite a yes. Not quite a no.

"That's a shame," Opal said. "She's ever so much nicer than Nina."

"*Everybody's* nicer than Nina," I said.

"They are, aren't they?" said Opal. "I've got my own netball in the cloakroom. Shall we go and get it?"

I didn't really want to play netball with Opal, but I didn't have the heart to say no. She was obviously lonely. She stuck with me all the rest of the day. She seemed to think that *she* was my best friend now.

Chapter 8
What's the Secret?

On Thursday I asked Mum if I could take my snow globe to school so that I could show it to my class.

"Well, I suppose," Mum said, "if you really want to. But remember, it's quite fragile. You'd better wrap it in something."

I lovingly wrapped it in cotton wool, stuck round with sticky tape, and then placed it very carefully in my school bag. I remembered what

Millie had said. *"We won't let people shake it cos we don't want it to get broken."* She probably wouldn't care now, if it did get broken. She might even think it served me right.

As I was on my way into school, Opal came bounding up to me. She almost crashed into my bag. She is rather a clumsy sort of person. Her arms and legs fly about all over the place.

I whisked the bag out of the way just in time. "Careful!" I said.

"Oops!" she said. "Sorry." And then she giggled and said, "What have you got in there?"

"It's my object," I said. "For English."

"Ooh!" Her eyes went big. "Is it something breakable?"

"It is if people go crashing into it," I said. I must have sounded a bit cross cos her face turned pink and she backed away. So then, of course, I felt mean. She can't help being clumsy.

"Do you want to take a peek?" I said. "Only you have to promise not to say anything when we read out our sentences."

She nodded, eagerly. "I promise!"

We didn't have English until later in the day, so at lunch time I left the snow globe in the tray under my desk. Millie stood watching me.

"Did you bring it?" she said. "Is that it?"

"Don't tell her," Opal cried.

Millie pulled a face. "Think I care?"

Just for a moment I hoped she did. But she turned and went running off after Marie and the others, and I was left with Opal.

Opal beamed at me. "It's our secret," she said. "Isn't it?"

From somewhere near by a voice said, "What is?"

We both spun round. *Yuck!* It was Nina Kirkby.

"So, what's the secret?" she said.

"If I told you," I said, "it wouldn't be a secret any more, would it?"

"It's rude to have secrets," Nina said.

"Too bad," I said.

I hoped that would get rid of her, but she stayed glued to my side all lunch time. There was just no way I could shake her off. Opal disappeared. I think she was a bit scared of Nina and her sharp tongue.

About five minutes before the bell rang, I began to worry about the snow globe. We're not supposed to leave valuables in the classroom. Not that the snow globe was *valuable*, exactly. I mean, it wasn't worth hundreds of pounds or anything. But stuff can get stolen. I couldn't bear it if anyone took Gran's snow globe.

As soon as the bell rang I went racing into school.

"What's the rush?" Nina called after me.

My snow globe! I'd promised Mum I would look after it. I should have put it in my locker or kept it with me or ... or –

"*Oh!*"

I skidded to a halt as I reached the classroom. Millie was in there. She was just moving away from my desk. She opened her mouth as if to say something, then snapped it back shut. Did she really look guilty, or was I just imagining it?

By now all the rest of the class were crowding in.

"Millie Jones, what are you doing in here?" Nina said. "You know we're not meant to be in school during the lunch break."

Millie didn't say anything. She just gave me this strange look and moved away.

Opal was hovering behind me. Someone shouted, "Watch it, you!" It was Dahlia. She gave Opal a shove, so that Opal almost fell on top of me and made me crash into my desk.

"Careful!" I said.

"Sorry," Opal whispered. "I'm sorry, I'm sorry!"

"That's OK," I said. "You couldn't help it."

And then I reached under my desk to check the snow globe. I knew at once that something terrible had happened. The cotton wool was just a sticky mess. My precious snow globe had been shattered!

Chapter 9
Real Friends

I stood there with my heart pounding and my hands all trembly. Millie was watching from across the room. Just for a moment, our eyes met and then, very deliberately, she turned away. She couldn't look at me.

Ms Hussein came in, and one after another we read out our sentences. I could hardly read for the wobble in my voice. It was Dahlia who guessed what my object was.

"It's one of those little globe things, isn't it?"

"Globe things with the snow," said Kevin.

At any other time I'd have been pleased that Kevin had spoken up. I'd have taken out my snow globe and given it him to hold.

"Abi, it sounds beautiful," Ms Hussein said. "Did you bring it with you?"

I shook my head and muttered that I had forgotten. Tears were prickling at the back of my eyes.

Ms Hussein said, "Well, that's a shame. I'd love to have seen it."

I sank back down at my desk. I thought it was odd that Opal hadn't said anything. *She* knew I hadn't forgotten. But she was just sitting there, at the desk next to mine, sucking at her thumb as if it was a dummy. It was then that I noticed – she was sucking her thumb cos it was bleeding. She must have cut it on something. And, suddenly, it came to me … *she* was the one who had broken my snow globe. It wasn't Millie at all. It was that stupid, clumsy Opal!

As the bell rang for afternoon break I leaned across and hissed, "It was you, wasn't it?"

She knew at once what I was talking about. She shrank back, looking scared.

"I'm sorry," she whispered. "I just wanted to have another look at it."

Out in the playground she did her best to cling to me, but I stomped away. I didn't want anything more to do with her. She'd broken Gran's snow globe and I wasn't ever going to forgive her.

To my surprise I found that Millie was waiting for me. "Did you *really* think I'd do something like that?" she said.

I fell silent. I couldn't think what to say.

"You did," Millie said, "didn't you? You thought it was me!"

"Only for a moment," I pleaded. "But I know now that it wasn't. It was Opal."

Millie said, "Oh! So *that's* why I bumped into her in the corridor. I wondered what she was doing. I just went back to make sure nobody had been to your desk. I knew you'd think I was guilty."

I hung my head. I was the one that was guilty. How could I ever have suspected Millie of doing anything so mean?

I waited for her to turn and walk off, but instead she gave me this sudden grin.

"Don't worry," she said. "If the police had been there they'd have arrested me."

"It's Opal they should arrest," I muttered.

"Are you going to report her?" said Millie.

I gazed at Opal across the playground. She was standing sadly by herself in her usual corner. I gave a big sigh and said, "She didn't do it on purpose. She just wanted to have another look at it. She's clumsy, that's all. Do you think we should go and talk to her?"

"About what?" said Millie.

"We could maybe ask her if she'd like to hang out with us?" I said.

"*Opal?*" Millie pulled a face. "When she's just broken our snow globe?"

"It's just that she looks so lonely," I said.

"Oh, I suppose," Millie said. "If you really want to."

"We don't have to," I said. "Not if *you* don't want to."

"You want to," said Millie. "That's what matters. If one of us really wants to do something, we do it. That's what being friends is about. Specially *best* friends."

I said, "Y-yes, but –"

"Oh, do come on," said Millie. She hooked her arm through mine. "If we're going to be friends, then let's be *real* friends!"

How to make your own snow globe

You will need ...

- An empty glass jar with a lid that fits well

- One or two small plastic figures to put in the jar. (They must be plastic so that they don't rust.)

- Strong, waterproof glue

- Tap water

- Glitter

- Glycerine, if you have some.

What you need to do ...

1. Take the lid off the jar and glue the plastic figure or figures to it. The lid will be the bottom of the snow globe, so make sure you glue the figures on the underneath of the lid.

2. When the glue is dry, fill the jar with water. If you can add a drop or two of glycerine to the water it will make the glitter fall more slowly.

3. Add 1 or 2 teaspoons of glitter.

4. Put some glue round the inside rim of the lid and screw the lid back on the jar. Make sure it is nice and tight.

5. Let the glue dry.

6. Turn the jar upside down and shake it. You have made a snow globe!

7. Now you can try making all different kinds of snow globes using different figures and different jars.

Our books are tested
for children and young people by
children and young people.

Thanks to everyone who consulted on
a manuscript for their time and effort in
helping us to make our books better
for our readers.